A Wish for You

Matt Novak

Greenwillow Books

An Imprint of HarperCollinsPublishers

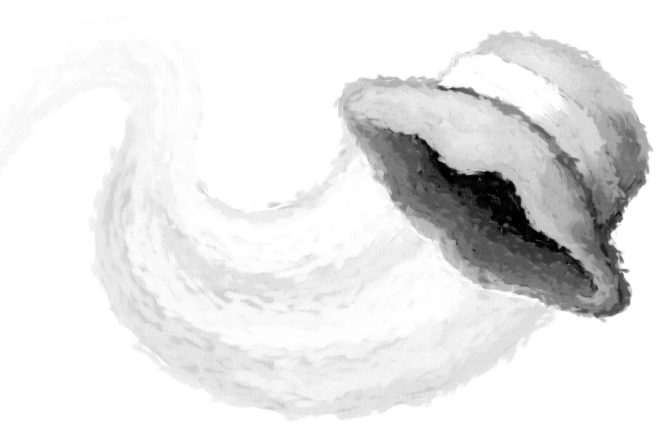

A Wish for You
Copyright © 2010 by Matt Novak
All rights reserved. Manufactured in China.
For information address HarperCollins Children's Books,
10 East 53rd Street, New York, NY 10022.
www.harpercollinschildrens.com

Digital art was used for the full-color art.
The text type is 44-point Else.

Library of Congress Cataloging-in-Publication Data

Novak, Matt.
A wish for you / by Matt Novak.
p. cm.
"Greenwillow Books."
Summary: A rhyming story with illustrations and simple text
celebrating the addition of a child to a family.
ISBN 978-0-06-155202-1 (trade bdg.)
[1. Stories in rhyme. 2. Family—Fiction. 3. Babies—Fiction.] I. Title.
PZ8.3.N8555Wi 2010   [E]—dc22   2008052485

10 11 12 13 LEO First Edition 10 9 8 7 6 5 4 3 2 1

 Greenwillow Books

To Victoria, Tabitha, and Sophia,

who have made all my wishes come true

Before there was you,

there was one . . .

and one,

then two.

Exploring the world

in a bright red canoe.

Two riding
yaks in
Timbuktu.

Two sometimes felt blue.

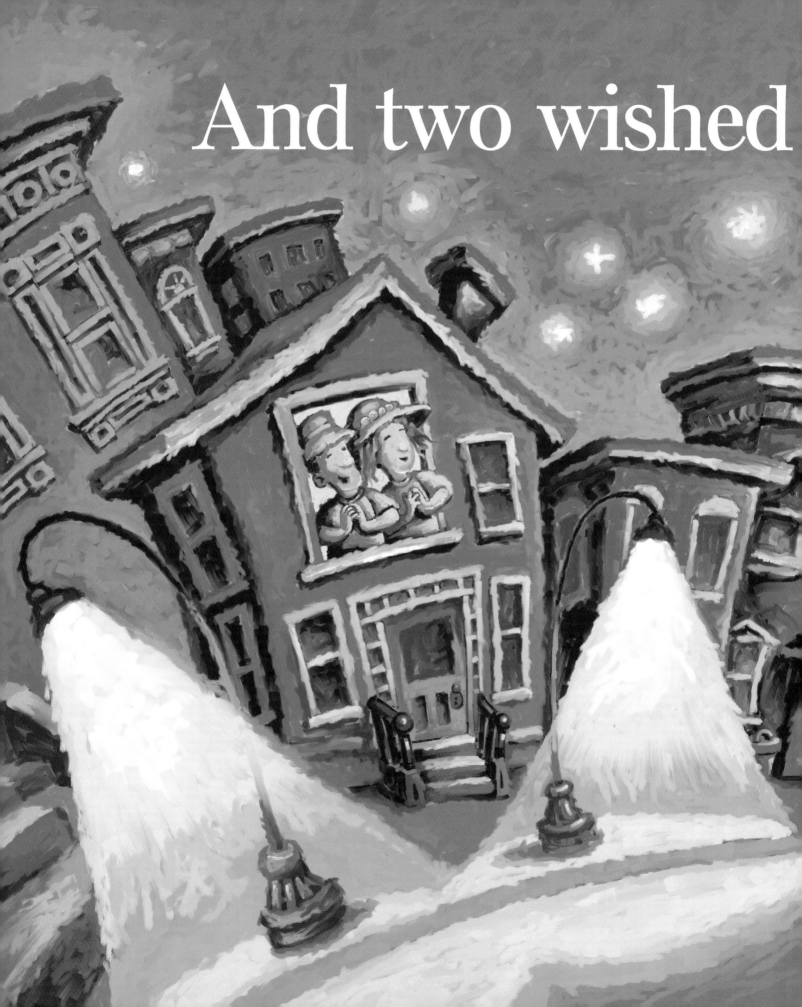

And two wished

for
you.

You grew

and grew!

Then there were two with so much to do.

Finally, the wish came true.

When you were new . . .

rock-a-bye

and

peek-a-boo.

Long sunny walks at the city zoo.

We're not just two.

We're three.